Animals Can Help

Written by Brylee Gibson

Rigby

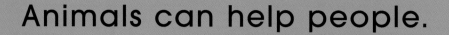

Animals can help people.

Dogs can help people.
Horses can help people.
Monkeys can help people, too.

2

This man cannot see.
He has a dog to help him.
The dog can help him go
over the road.

This man cannot get
the phone.
The dog can help him.
The dog can get
the phone for him.

This woman cannot walk.
The dog can help
this woman.
The dog can make
the light go on and off.

9

This boy cannot walk.
He can sit on the horse
and the horse can walk.

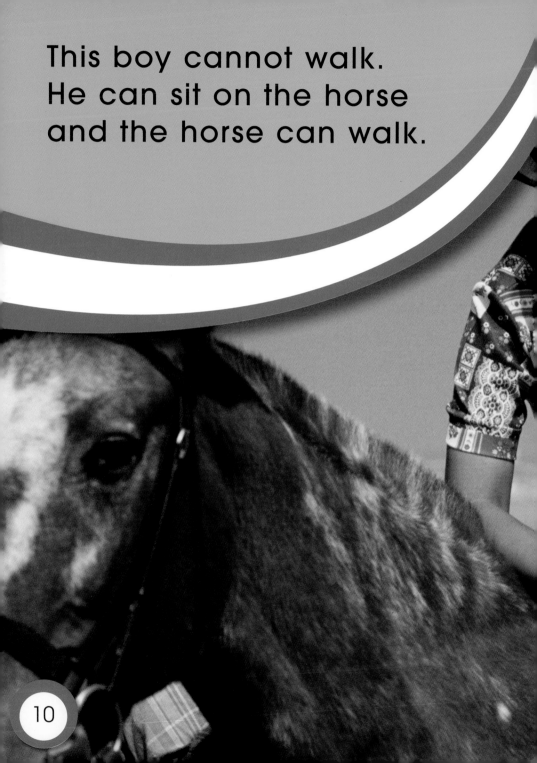

This woman cannot move.
The monkey can help her.
It can wash her face.

It can clean
the floor.

The monkey can open the refrigerator. It can help the man have a drink, too.

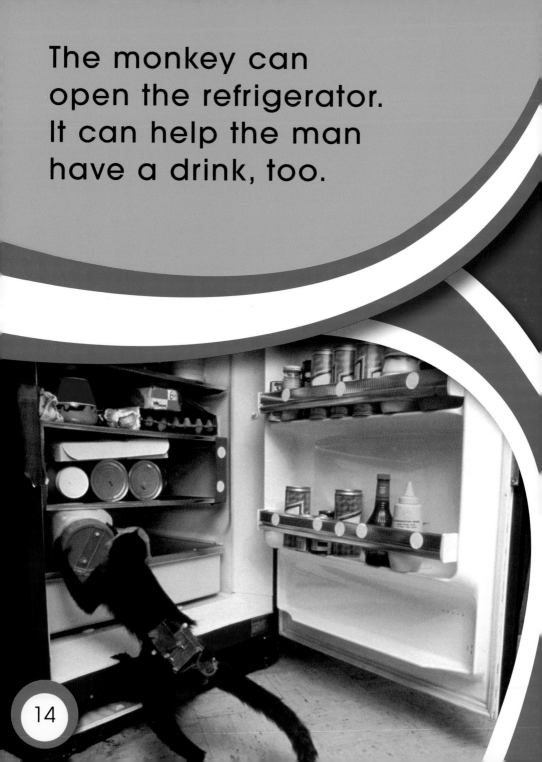

Index

Guide Notes

Title: Animals Can Help

Stage: Early (2) – Yellow

Genre: Nonfiction

Approach: Guided Reading

Processes: Thinking Critically, Exploring Language, Processing Information

Written and Visual Focus: Photographs (static images), Index

Word Count: 125

THINKING CRITICALLY
(sample questions)

- Look at the title and read it to the children. Ask the children what they know about animals that help people.
- Focus the children's attention on the index. Ask: "What are you going to find out about in this book?"
- If you want to find out about dogs helping people, which pages would you look on?
- If you want to find out about monkeys helping people, which pages would you look on?
- How do you think animals might learn to help people?
- Why do you think a monkey would be a good animal to help people?

EXPLORING LANGUAGE

Terminology
Title, cover, photographs, author, photographers

Vocabulary
Interest words: phone, light, refrigerator, floor, face, wash
High-frequency words: make, her
Positional words: on, off

Print Conventions
Capital letter for sentence beginnings, periods, commas